ARON NELS STEINKE

THE SUPER-DUPER DOG PARK

BALLOON TOONS®

🍎 BLUE APPLE BOOKS

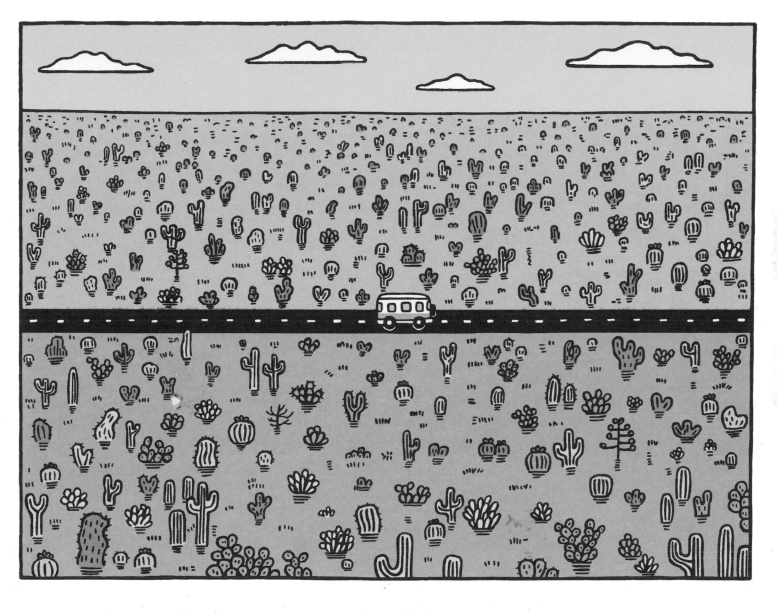

BOUNCE HOUSE

WE'RE GOING SOMEPLACE SPECIAL...

LET'S INVITE OUR FRIENDS!

FOR RENFIELD

Published in the United States 2011 by

Blue Apple Books

515 Valley Street, Maplewood, NJ 07040

www.blueapplebooks.com

First Edition 08/11
Printed in China
HC ISBN: 978-1-60905-093-1
2 4 6 8 10 9 7 5 3 1
PB ISBN: 978-1-60905-184-6
2 4 6 8 10 9 7 5 3 1